A PART OF THE GAME

A Part Of The Game

ISBN 978-1-365-60578-9

Kasper Hoe

A Part of the Game
(5 dark tales)

For Helen;

Thanks for helping me on this project.
Seems like it actually *was* just A Part Of The Game.

Content

Foreword

This book was originally published as an E-book. But this printed edition has a bonus story; "Price Of Lust.

I decided to republish this little collection of dark tales, because I realized that it would be much better in print in stead of reading it on a screen.

The tales have been on a kind of a journey lately; first they were written by me, then they went to Canada for a check-up by my friend, Helen Joan Vandepeer, who checked it for small mistaking details, and at last they ended up in your hands. I hope, you're going to enjoy them.

I wondered if I should put some notes about the tales into this foreword, but I decided that I wouldn't, because I wouldn't risk that I would make spoilers in stead of teasers.

After all, that would be like people talking about movies, and before you even see the movie, you know the ending, because those people make spoilers in stead of teasers.

Kasper Hoe.

A part of the game

”If you look behind you, you will not be able to see me,” the voice said in the phone, “I’m there but there are so many people behind you so you will not be able to see me.”
”Who are you?” Janice asked anxiously.
”That is exactly the question,” the voice replied.
The only thing Janice knew for certain was that the voice belonged to a man.
”By the way, Janice, if you ever find me, you may still not be sure that it is the right person you have found.”
”You know what?” Janice was getting annoyed,
“This is a bad joke. The worst joke ever.”
”Joke?” the voice became sinister,
“Who’s joking? Do you think I sound like a joker?”
Janice looked over her left shoulder. The voice was right. There were many people behind her.

Many of them did also talk in the mobile phone.
"Janice?" the voice asked, "Are you still there?"
"Won't you give me a hint?" she asked, "Just something?"
"About what?"
"You," she replied, "Who the hell are you?"
"Janice," the voice said, "Neither Heaven nor Hell belong in this conversation. If you want a tip, I can tell you that I am a man."
"Yes, I've just found out," Janice snapped, "and to me, you sound like a perverted pig."
She hung up, but a few seconds later, the phone rang again in her pocket.
"Janice?" the voice said when she answered the call.
"What the hell are you playing at, you pig?" Janice had trouble controlling her voice.
"We've got a little problem here," he sounded calm and collected.
"Well," she replied, "and what kind of a problem might that be?"
"Your behavior."
"Fuck you, you bastard!" She

shouted into the phone.
"You see?" the voice remained calm, "Your behavior and your language are both the problems here."
"What the hell is it that you want?"
"Janice," the voice answered, "as mentioned earlier, God, Satan, Heaven, or Hell doesn't belong in this little game. But now, when you ask, I'll tell you what I want."
"What?"
"I want you to go into the cafe, located on the other side of the street, "the Country Corner Cafe."
Janice looked around, and just on the other side of the road, the cafe was located.
"Yeah, okay," she said and hung up.
When she entered the cafe, the bartender asked:
"What would it be, Miss?"
"Just a cup of coffee, please."
"Certainly," the bartender said and started to make a cup of coffee for Janice.
The bartender was dressed in a way

that suited excellently to the scene; he was wearing a white shirt and western necktie that looked like one of those you can see in Tombstone with Kurt Russell. Oh yes, and he had cowboy boots on. They seemed made of snakeskin.

She got her coffee.

"Here you go, ma'am."

Janice was just about to sip the coffee when her phone rang again.

"Well done, Janice," the voice said, "you completed the first part, without major problems. Can you see that you are cooperating when you're under pressure?"

"Will you please leave me now?" Janice asked, and hoped fervently that the man on the phone would hang up and just disappear from her life and stay away.

"No," the voice replied, "for now we are going. The game is running and you do it so well."

"What game?"

"You'll see," the voice replied, "just stay there and see what happens."

While Janice sat and sipped coffee, she saw a guy who sat at the other end of the bar, where he intensely followed her with his eyes. She chose to ignore him and looked away. After some time he came down to her and asked:
”Do you know that you are a good looking chick?”
Janice did not answer.
”My name is Drake,” the guy continued, “what’s your name?”
She still didn’t answer.
”Hello, darling, I'm talking to you.”
Janice rose without a word and walked out of the café, and the guy followed her.
”Hello!” he shouted, “Can’t you just tell me your name? I just wanted to talk!”
Janice went on without a word and without turning around.
”Janice! Damn it!”
Janice stopped abruptly. She was deeply surprised. She turned and started walking back toward the café. Along the way she had only *one* thought, one urgent question: she blurted it out immediately.

"How do you know my name?"
He smiled sheepishly and looked almost like a person who had been drinking all afternoon.
"I just know," he replied as he stood and rocked in imitation of Johnny Depp in the role as Jack Sparrow.
"From where?"
"Well"; he answered; "now you will talk."
Janice sighed.
"Just tell me how you know my name," she said in an almost begging tone.
"It's just part of the game."
It startled her. That was the answer that she did *not* like. There was something sinister about it. Just as with the voice of the strange calls.
"What'd you say?" She asked.
"It's a part of the game," Drake repeated, "was the answer I should give you, if you asked."
"Who told you that?"
"The voice," he replied.
"The voice from the phone calls?" Janice asked.
Drake nodded.

"What else did you know?" Janice asked.

He looked hard at her face, evaluating what he should say, how much he could tell her.

"That a young woman would enter the café," he replied, "and that I should score her."

"Score her?" Asked Janice surprised, "If it's me, I am very sorry, but I am not a single."

"That is not true," Drake said, "I know that you and your boyfriend broke up fourteen days ago. So you are a single. You're just trying to get rid of me so I cannot fulfill my part of the game."

"How do you know that?"

"The voice told me. And my job actually sounded a few more things."

"I am not sure I want to hear the rest," Janice said.

Drake laughed lustful and answered:

"Oh, believe me, you will."

"With the response and the playful laughter, I think any time I am free."

"Oh, beauty," Drake said in an

almost apologetic tone, "let us now get to know each other. What do you say to come visiting me? I live right here behind the café."
"No thanks."
"So let me at least see you again," Drake said.
She stood and looked as if she really was considering the proposal carefully.
"Maybe, if you forget about all those comments about scoring me. You are not exactly my type."
"What's your type?" Drake asked and seemed genuinely interested in hearing the answer, "To be honest, do you really know the answer to that question?"
Janice pondered the question carefully before she answered resignedly:
"No, okay. But I just can't imagine the two of us together. Not that way anyway. By the way, we don't even know one another."
"Exactly," replied Drake, "then let us know each other."
"Maybe later," said Janice, "but I do not have time now. I've got to run."

When Janice had come away from the café, she heard Drake shout:
”See you, beautiful!”
”Yes,” Janice shouted back, though she inwardly had this burning feeling that she wished she had never met Drake, and that she would never get to meet him again.

When Janice had entered the front door that led into the stairwell where her apartment was, her cell phone rang again.
”Janice,” the voice said at the other end, “that’s not the right attitude to end the day on, when the first part of the game was done so well.”
”What are you talking about?” She asked, sounded like she had no idea what the voice had earlier mentioned about the game.
”You know what I mean,” the voice answered, “and Drake, you were so dismissive of, is actually a nice guy. He knows the rules of the game and knows what is expected of him.”
Janice began to get a sickening feeling that the sick motherfucker

on the phone was more sick and bizarre than even the sickest movie villain, she had seen. Even Freddy Krueger was water on the side, because this was *real*. It was *her* reality.
She locked herself into the apartment and said:
"I don't have time now." She ended the conversation and rushed out to the bathroom, knocked the toilet seat up and vomited.
- "Fuck, this is sick," - she thought as she flushed the toilet ball and stood on rather unsteady legs.
She looked in the mirror, her face was white, and her hands shook.
While she stood there, her thoughts circled on the voice from the calls, which, incidentally, was from a hidden number, and Drake.
- The game, - she thought, - it's all about the game. But exactly *what* game, is it about? -
At the same moment an SMS beeped into her mobile phone.
'*My game.*'
The sender of the message had been

smart enough to send the message from an SMS service on the Internet.
- How can he answer me a question I just thought? - and she felt a nauseating feeling come again. This seriously began to be sinister.
She suddenly had the thought that she had to do with a guy who was actually able to read her thoughts without seeing her simultaneously.

Later, as evening darkened the sky outside, she decided that she would not get to grips with making an entire game meal just for herself.
- It was something else, while Martin was also a part of it here, - she thought, - but what do I find for dinner? -
She did not last very long above the answer before she made herself comfortable in front of her computer.
- I just order something, - she thought, - a little self-indulgence doesn’t matter occasionally. -

She logged onto her account on justeat.com where she ordered a Mexican with extra chili and garlic, a half-liter of cola, a Cheese 'N' Bacon burger for delivery. No, a little self-indulgence didn’t matter, and it was just what she wanted.
She entered that she would like it to be delivered as soon as possible, because she was just as hungry as if she could have eaten half a cow, if not a whole one.
When she was finished entering the information she needed on the page, she logged of her Just-eat account, got up and walked over to the stereo, where she quickly found a CD to put on.
Despite her experience from earlier that day, down at Café Country Corner, she chose to put a CD on with the Oaks Ville Country Band. She'd certainly have nothing against country music. No, it was actually some pretty good music. She especially liked Dolly Parton's *I Will Always Love You* which Whitney Houston sang in The Bodyguard. Oh yes, and she also

liked Kenny Rogers and Johnny Cash. But there was something special about Dolly Parton.

She sat down on the couch, lit a cigarette, and enjoyed the first puff. She looked around the room, where she had a standard lamp with dimmed lights, so it was nice subdued. Not too pervasive, nor gloomy. No, it was just perfectly lit.

Since there had been little time, it rang at the door. It was Murat, who was tender with her stud pizzeria Abdul Pizza & Grill. He smiled his usual smile as she opened the door.

Janice had always thought that Murat looked so cute when he smiled. She could not really explain it, but there was something charming about his smile. When she got the food, which she had ordered, and she had paid, Murat said:

”Are you in town tonight?”

She shrugged.

”Come on, Janie,” he said.

Murat had called her Janie since the final years of school. He had

told an interesting girl might have an interesting nickname. And ever since then, he had called her Janie.
”I'll consider it,” she replied, “but I had considered staying at home with either a good book or a movie.”
”I hope you come in town,” said Murat, “The Oaks Ville Country Band plays at Country Corner tonight.”

Shit, he knew exactly what he should say to entice her to go out in the city that night, where she perhaps ought to guard against it. She did so reluctantly encounter Drake.

”I'll consider it,” she replied.

After eating, Janice leaned back on the couch, grabbed the cigarette pack, and lit a cigarette.
- Oaks Ville Country Band comes to town, - she thought.
She was actually quite tempted by Murat's invitation. But on the

other hand, she had no desire to encounter Drake down at Country Corner, and something indicated that it was his parent place.

At that moment the phone rang.

”Just take off,” the voice said, “I’ve done, so you can enjoy your music tonight.”

”What do you mean?” Janice asked wondering, “What’s going on?”

There was a split second of silence before the voice replied: ”I have suspended the game until tomorrow.”

It was wonderful to hear. Maybe even to wonderful though. Janice hesitated. She doubted whether she could trust the voice or not. Her mother had always - at least since Janice was 16 years old - said that she should beware of relying on strangers. These words convinced her.

”And how can I be sure that it is not just something you say to make it easy to Drake to fulfill his part of the game?” she asked, “How do I know, if he leaves me alone or not? How can I be sure that you leave me alone?”

There was a moment where there was completely quiet in the other end of the line.
”I promise you that the game is set for tomorrow,” the voice said then, ”and I promise you that Drake leaves you alone until the game continues again. So just go and listen to the country music, Janice.”
The voice hung up, and Janice was now left with considering whether she should go or whether she should stay home. Certainly she wanted to leave. Partly because she wanted to hear Oaks Ville Country Band lives on stage, but also because she wanted to meet up with Murat.
- I’ll do it, - she thought, - by God in heaven, I’ll do it. Admittedly, I was told that the game continues tomorrow, but I cannot ruin my evening. I will not let the game thing ruin my evening. -

When Janice, thirteen minutes later, went in through the door down at the Country Corner, Murat

came immediately towards her and hugged her gently and amicable. Somehow, she would not have objected, if he had put a little more than just friendship in the hug. For from Murat only, she would have liked a little more than just a friendly hug.
”Hey, beautiful,” he said, “you look great.”
She blushed slightly. Probably mainly because of the sweet smile, he sent her when he said it.
”I have not otherwise done so much out of it,” she replied modestly.
”Hey, Janie,” he said, “In my eyes you are always good looking. I thought, you knew.”
Oh, he was so cute. She could not resist the charm of his. It might be something very special for a guy like him, because she had not actually experienced it at some other guy, as long as she could remember.
She thanked him and smiled discreetly.
At 10 pm, Oaks Ville Country Band walked on stage. Janice hoped that they would play a few exceptional

songs that night. She had heard their copy version of Dolly Parton's *Stand by Your Man*, and it was one of the songs she especially hoped that they would perform that night. Not because she had a man to stick to, but maybe she would have it later. Something inside her was hoping it more than it ever did before.
When the band had played for three quarters, the lead singer said that there was a break in which the bartender turned the jukebox on. That evening they didn't spare the country music. During intermission were both played ”San Quentin” by Johnny Cash and some Christian country music, as Janice didn't remember the names of the artists on.
On the whole there was a pretty cool feeling on the spot. People were dressed up in their best country style with cowboy hats, cowboy boots, and western shirts with neckties. And by some of the tables around, elder men sat and smoked small cigars, which almost got them to look like Clint

Eastwood in *The Good, the Bad, and the Ugly*.

"When they come back on stage again, can I have the next dance?" Murat asked.

Janice smiled and nodded.

"Yes, of course you can."

He thanked honorably, as though he had expected that she would have answered no.

When the break had lasted for fifteen minutes, the guitarist came back on stage, took the guitar in his arms, and began to tune it and then he started playing the anthem of "Amazing Grace", which actually sounded pretty well. When he'd played the anthem three times, the singer came up on stage and she began to sing it. It sounded really great, and she just hit the high notes perfectly.

When they had finished the song, the second department started in earnest.

"And now," the singer said, "we have a little quiet ballad to the people who are in love. There may be many of those here at Country

Corner tonight."
They began to play *I will always love you*, which was one of Janice's favorite songs. As she was musing over the song, Murat said:
"Wasn't there something about a dance?"
She blushed gently and replied:
"Yes, that's true. Sorry, I was about to forget it. "
"it's okay," Murat said understanding, "if you'd rather wait until next issue, that's okay, too."
She shook her head.
"No, that's not the reason," she replied, "come and dance with me before I regret it."
She smiled and winked at him.
They danced through the rest of the song, and she enjoyed it more than she had expected that she would get to. She had not danced with some guy since the night when she was started dating Martin. But dancing with Murat was actually really pleasant. And she almost felt it being quite romantic.
Maybe it had something to do with

the played song. But it was certainly wonderful.
”Will you go home with me afterwards and have a glass of wine?” She asked him.
He looked at her with a look that asked if she really was sure it was a good idea, which caused her to hesitate a little at the invitation. She wanted to, but if he wouldn’t, she couldn’t really do or say anything about it.
”I would really like to,” he replied, “but I don’t hope that you stop dancing until the song ends just because of the wine. I am not thirsty enough to let a glass of wine spoil my first dance with you.”

About half an hour later, they both sat at Janice’s place. The lights were subdued a bit more than it had been while she ate the dinner, which Murat had brought to her earlier that evening. There was soft music on the stereo. It was not country music, but it was quite appropriate for the occasion anyway. And she had lit a few candles that stood and burned on the coffee table.

”You live pretty nice here,” Murat said, as he put his wine glass on the table.

She smiled.

”I am also quite happy with this flat,” she replied, "I just have got the space I need. Yes, actually there is a little more than I need when I'm alone.”

”Well, I am sorry that you and Martin broke up,” Murat said almost apologetically, "I never really thought that you would fall apart that way.”

It was nice to know that Murat was so sympathetic towards her, because he had actually been a really close friend of both her and Martin. But after Martin progressed, it was a bit like Murat had taken her party. Okay, so it was not *her* who had committed the gaffe, which had caused that they were not even parted as friends.

”No, but that was certainly evident,” she said.

She was actually recovered quite

quickly over the break up with Martin. Had it been a week earlier, she might have begun crying over the fact that Murat had brought the breach into the conversation. But after the piece of shit, Martin had done after the breakup she didn't really think about him anymore.
"How are you?" Murat asked, "I have not really had a good opportunity to ask you."
She smiled and answered softly:
"It's alright. I'm fine enough with it. So, I speak neither with him or her more. But I feel fine enough."
"You also dropped being in touch with her?" Murat asked.
"Yes, of course," she replied, "there are always two for a Tango. And it was not a rape or something like that. They were two on doing it and they were both deleted from my list of friends."
Murat nodded understanding.
"What now?"
She shrugged.

"Is there another in the

binoculars?”

She pulled her shoulders and began to tell:

”During yesterday, I had got a lot of calls from a voice that I cannot place. He talks about some games. And then he got a guy named Drake to come in at the Country Corner and proposition me yesterday’s afternoon.”

It startled Murat.

”Did you say Drake?” Murat asked, “Janie, whatever may happen… No matter how desperate you are to find a new guy, so check back for God's sake, away from Drake.”
”Why?” Asked Janice “Is he really that bad?”
Murat looked like someone who was about to get up from the couch and run away, while the opportunity was there.
”It is very much worse,” Murat answered, “Don’t you read newspapers?”
Janice looked at Murat.

"What is it, Mullet?" She asked, "Why do you react like this?"

"Drake is a womanizer of the ugly kind," said Murat, "and when I say the ugly kind, I don't mean by the looks. He is not content just to flirt. He goes further. "

"Isn't that a supposed part on scoring?"

"Janie, I do not think you understand where I want to lead you. Sometimes, he goes so far that he is not only the next guy on the girls' lists of boyfriends. Sometimes, he's also the last."

"What do you mean?" Janice asked.

"Now, I rather understand what you were talking about," Murat said continuing, "the thing about the game is just that you should be next on his list."

"Well, the voice from the calls is not Drake," Janice said.

"No," Murat said applying, "but believe me, this is what the game is about. I've heard about the game before, and I have also lost some friends to Drake through the game. And I will not lose you too."

"Well, what can we do to avoid it?" Janice asked.
"We must play our game with *them*, as they play theirs with you," said Murat, "and if it becomes the last thing I do, I will do my best to stop the people who are doing this to you. I will do as much as I can to make them leave you in peace."

When they had emptied the first bottle of wine, Murat asked:
"May I borrow the toilet?"
"Yes, of course," Janice answered, "it's the door right away in the hall."
When Murat was gone into the bathroom and the door clicked as it was locked Janice's mobile phone rang.
"You're not alone," the voice said, "I know you're not."
"And how do you know that?"
"You refused Drake for a Pizza delivery guy," the voice said with a hint of mockery in his voice, "a fucking jack-in-a-hurry-boy from the Middle East."
"You did not answer my question,"

Janice noted and tried to sound triumphant.
The voice paused for a moment, and then he replied:
"I don't need to answer your questions. The game is started again and I have chosen my next move."
"And what is *that*?" Janice asked.
The male voice hung up, and Janice sat back staring at the phone when Murat came back from the toilet.
"What's going on, Janie?" He asked.
Janice did not answer, but just sat and looked at the phone.
"Was it him?"
"He knows you're here," she answered, "but how he knows it, he wouldn't tell."
Murat sat down with a sigh.
"You want me to leave?"
For the first time after the call, she looked at him as she replied:
"No, I would actually prefer that you stay with me. Because when you're near, I feel safe."
He smiled and put his right arm around her.
"If you feel more comfortable with

it, I will gladly stay."

In the same second, the phone rang again, and Janice was going to answer it, as Murat said:

"Let me handle this."

She handed him the phone and he answered the call.

"Janice is a part of the game," the voice said, "let me talk to her."

"You can't, because she's not here right now," Murat answered and sat quite relaxed.

"You lie, jack-in-a-hurry-boy," the voice hissed on the phone, "I know she is sitting right beside you. So let me talk to her."

"Don't you understand what I'm telling you?" Murat asked, "I tell you that you can't talk with her now."

"I'll tell you something, Pizza delivery guy," the voice continued, "if you hope to get some juicy pussy tonight, then drop it. She is nothing but a little pussy fool."

Murat clenched his teeth in fury.

"Could you speak very well nicely, you perverted pig?"

”Oh,” the voice said condescendingly, “Is the little black dude getting angry now?”
Murat could feel the anger grow inside him, and his temples began to cans, while the anger rose.
”Just leave her alone,” he said doggedly, “and be careful, maybe you're pissing off the wrong person.”
The voice was silent a moment.
”I think it's you and the little bitch who should be careful,” the voice said then, ”the game has begun, and I've found my next move.”

That night was the first in which Janice had a guy with her, since she and Martin had broken up. She didn’t certainly feel bad about it, because Martin was too far out of the picture, and Murat was such a nice guy.
There was no love making in the picture, for Janice had the principle that she didn’t have sex with a guy on first date. But there were long rolls of kissing, and Murat was an amazing kisser.

Suddenly, as the night had passed, it was probably around three in the morning, her mobile rang.
”Do you still have a visitor?” the voice asked, “Yes, you know, since the plug-in-rend-boy hopes to get in your panties during the night. But we are moving towards the grand finale.
”Get lost,” said Janice, “and leave us alone.”
The voice laughed at the other end.
”It will be interesting to see how the finale ends,” he said, ”but whatever the outcome will be, I want you to know that you have been a really interesting girl to have in the game.”
”What the hell are you talking about a finale?” she asked and looked at Murat, who was lying beside her.
”You and the jack-in-run-boy will soon get to see what I’m talking about,” the voice answered, ”perhaps the pizza delivery guy knows what I'm talking about. Just ask him, if he remembers some of the others.”

The voice hung up, and Janice looked intensely at Murat, who looked baffled back at her.
"What's going on, Janie?" he asked.
"He spoke of a finale," she replied, "does that mean anything to you? He told me to ask you, if you remembered some of the others."
Murat sighed.
"Do you remember what I told you earlier?" he asked, "About the friends I'd lost in their game?"
Janice nodded. Actually, she remembered that she had noticed that Murat had been looking very depressed, as he had told her.
"Initially, they did very well," Murat continued, "but unlike you, they fell into Drake's trap. And when they had reached the finals, where Drake would give the decision, it turned out that these girls did not escape alive. He murdered them with his sick game."
"What's that kind of finale?" she asked, "How does it work?"
Murat sighed. His eyes were wet by tears which he wiped away with the

back of his hand before he replied:
"Unless it's changed, it's something with that guy who is in the game, choosing who should survive and die; him or the girl."
She looked astonished at him.
"Well, when I refused Drake," she said, "so there is hardly any doubt about what he chooses."
Murat looked deeply into her eyes.
"I'm not sure that Drake is the one who plays the decisive role anymore," he said.
"But who is it?" Janice asked surprised.
Murat sighed and wiped his eyes again.
"I'm afraid that it will be *me* this time."
"What are you saying?" she asked.
"You refused Drake for me," said Murat, "and since you are a girl who is a part of the game, it will probably be me, to be faced with the choice of whether you or I must get out of the game alive."

Two hours later, somebody rang on the door bell. Janice, who was not the type who opened the door for anyone, looked through the spy hole. There was totally dark in the hallway, so it was hard to see who stood out there. So she was obliged to open the door.

"Hi, Janice," the guy who stood on the ledge said, "It's time for the grand finale."

Janice hurried to close the door, but the guy reached out to use his foot as a door blocker.

"There is no point, Janice," he said, "this is a part of the game, and you can't escape."

The guy pushed the door open with such strength that Janice was pushed back until she stumbled across the boots she had been wearing at the evening when she was down at the Country Corner. He'd crushed in and stood and looked at Janice, who was lying on the entrance floor, wearing her pajamas only.

"Nice rig," the guy said, "and what a beautiful place you have here."

Janice had fought her way up again, and she asked:

"What the hell are you up to, you sick motherfucker?"
The guy smiled awry.
"Janice, I have told you that the devil has nothing to do with this game," he said, "but I'm going to complete the game. So now I think that you should go and tell the jack-in-rend-boy to come in here."
Janice was not exactly comfortable about what was happening. She would ideally have preferred that Murat should not be pulled into this hell.
"Go and get him," the guy said, "he has a finale waiting."
Janice shook her head and begged the guy to keep Murat out of this shit.
"I would really like to," the guy answered, "but you rummaged him into it."
"I am very sorry," Janice said, "I did not know. But for God's sake, let him go."
"I have said that God does not have a damn thing to do with this stuff!" the guy yelled, "And then get the fucking errand boy, you little bitch!"

Reluctantly Janice went into the bedroom where Murat was. He had heard every word.
"It's time," she whispered, "the guy from the calls is here, and the grand finale has arrived."
Murat was out of bed, walked towards her and took her in his arms.
"Just let me fix it," he whispered softly, "everything is going to be just fine."
They walked together into the living room where the guy was waiting for them.
"Oh my," he said, "Look at it; the jack-in-a-hurry-boy and the bitch."
He laughed. It was not a typical laughter, as you often hear when people laugh at a joke. No, this laughter was cruel, cold, and disgusting.
"Leave Janice alone," Murat said, "I've warned you."
The guy did not seem as if this warning made a big impression on him, quite the contrary.
"We'll see who I'll leave alone and which one I'm not," the guy

answered, ″it's really up to you, dear Pizza delivery guy.″
The guy smiled an eerie and cold smile.
″I already made my choice,″ Murat said, "I sacrifice myself for you to leave Janice alone.″
Janice grabbed his arm.
″No, Mullet,″ she exclaimed and began to cry, "You mustn't do that.″
Murat looked at her, wiped the tears away from her cheeks, and said:
″It's best that way. I will not let him hurt you.″
″But there must surely be a way out,″ Janice cried begging.
The guy looked at Janice evaluating.
″There is not,″ he said then, "it's either you or him. That is the rules of the game.″
The guy looked at Murat.
″What do you say, Pizza Delivery?″ he asked.
Murat kissed Janice, looked at the guy, and replied:
″Take me instead, and leave Janice alone.″

The guy folded his hands.
"Very well, Jack-in-a-hurry-boy," he said, "Then come with me. Party time has come."
The guy and Murat both disappeared out the door, and Janice was left behind. She was both relieved and distressed at the same time. She had lost Murat, but on the other hand, she escaped from more calls from the voice. No calls, she never heard from the voice again.

Game Over???

Fourteen days later, the eighteen year old Sabrina was out shopping at the local mall, when her cell phone rang...

The musical box

It was a wonderful, old piece, a fantastic toy that she had inherited from her grandmother, an antique musical box.
It was really well-kept in-spite of its age.
The grandmother had it since she was a child and she inherited it from her grandmother.
"But you should only use it by daylight," the grandmother said, when she gave it to Julie.
Julie didn't understand why she was only allowed to use it by daylight.
"There's something mysterious about it," the grandmother said, "so you must promise me, Julie, that you only use it by daylight."
"In what way is it mysterious?" Julie asked.
The grandmother sighed.
"When I was at your age," she said, "my grandmother gave this musical box to me. And she told me that she'd heard about a girl who used it just before she was going to sleep. Nobody ever saw the girl

again."
"What happened to the girl?" Julie asked.
"Nobody knows," said the grandmother, "but my grandmother told me it is damned. By daylight it can't hurt you. But if you use it between sunset and sunrise you're lost. Then you will be in its power."
Julie started laughing.
"Grandmother," she said, "I don't believe in things like that."
The grandmother looked seriously at Julie without smiling.
"Don't you believe what I tell you?" she asked.
"Yes, I use to," Julie said, "but a story like this one about a damned musical box. You might be able to do it better than that."
The grandmother shook her head sadly.
"Oh dear," she said, "you young ones don't believe things like that, do you? What you can't see does not exist. Isn't that the present young ones' view on life?"
"I don't know," Julie answered and pulled up her mobile phone.

She had an SMS.
The grandmother went to the kitchen.
"Are you hungry, Julie?" she asked.
"Yes," Julie answered.
When the grandmother had cut some pieces of bread, found the butter and the cheese, she came back to the dinner table.
"So," she said, "help yourself, dear."
"Thanks, grandma," Julie said and smiled.
"Oh, I forgot," the grandmother exclaimed, "do you want a fizzy drink?"
"Yes, thanks," Julie said, and the grandmother went to the fridge to get a fizzy drink for Julie.
"It's coke, you use to drink isn't it?" the grandmother asked from the kitchen.
"Yes," Julie answered, "but if you don't have it I can drink orange too."
The grandmother came back with a coke and placed it on the table, in front of Julie.
Julie took the grandmother's hand

and said:
"I'm sorry, that I didn't believe the story about the musical box."
The grandmother sighed and kissed Julie's forehead.
"Don't apologize, Julie," she said, "I understand why you don't believe it. It sounds like some made-up nonsense."
Julie said that it just sounded too fantastic to be true.
"I felt it the same way," the grandmother said when she got back to her chair.
"Grandma," Julie said, "have you ever used it after sunset?"
The grandmother shook her head and answered:
"No, I haven't. And I hope you'll never do it either. It can have such terrible consequences."
"The girl who disappeared," Julie asked, "was she in our family?"
"No, but my grandmother bought it from a second-hand dealer, who had it delivered just a few weeks after the girl disappeared."
Julie asked if the musical box wasn't just damned to people who believed it.

"I guess it would have better chances to trap people who don't believe it," the grandmother answered.
The grandmother poured out a cup of coffee and took a piece of bread with cheese.
"But it plays such a cute melody," she said.
Julie asked which melody it played.
"Red River Girl," the grandmother answered.
"Is that cute?" Julie asked, "I think it's boring."
The grandmother shook her head and asked.
"Didn't you ever realize how beautiful the lyrics are?"
"No, because I'm more up to some modern music instead of such old music," Julie answered.
"Old?" the grandmother asked, "Maybe it's old but not that old that you never hear it anymore. And by the way I think it's beautiful, and we don't have to agree with each other about that."
They both smiled at each other.

It was time for Julie to go home. She hardly reached the door before her grandmother stopped her.
“Julie,” she said, “Don’t forget your musical box.”
“That’s right,” Julie said, “I’d better remember that.”
She kissed her grandmother’s cheek and said:
“See you, grandma.”
“Come home safely,” the grandmother said, “and say hello to your mum for me.”

Half an hour later when Julie came home, her mother asked from the living room:
“Julie, is that you?”
“Yes, mum, it’s me,” Julie said, “and grandma told me to say hello.”
“Thank you, honey,” the mother said, “was she in a good mood?”
“Isn’t she always?” Julie asked.
“When I was at her place last time, she said something an old musical box,” the mother said, “Did you get it?”
Julie nodded, and her mobile phone rang.

It was her friend, Lucy, who called to invite Julie in for a "girls' night."

"Who else are coming?" Julie asked.

"Nana and Linda," Lucy answered.

"Okay," Julie said, "I'll be there in an hour."

Julie went to her room and put the musical box on a shelf.

"Damned?" she muttered, "yeah right."

She packed some stuff in a bag; lipstick, eyeliner, mascara and stuff like that. It happened from time to time, when they had "girls' night" at Lucy's place that they went to town later at night.

Julie closed the bag and went out the room. On her way out she looked at the musical box.

She nodded her head and closed the door behind her.

"I'll go to see Lucy," she said to her mother, who was watching the News.

"Okay," the mother said, "have a good time then."

"Thanks," Julie said and went out

the door.

Later when Julie and her friends were at Lucy's they were preparing themselves for the night in town.
"Where are we going tonight?" Linda asked.
Nana suggested that they should go to Bob's, a wine bar in town.
"No, I don't like that," Lucy said, "there's no cute guys to look at."
"Snow Queen?" Julie suggested.
They all agreed.
Julie reached down into her bag to get her lipstick. But it was something else she caught; the musical box.
"Wow," Nana said, "it's beautiful."
"Yeah, where did you get it?" Linda asked.
"I had it from my grandma," Julie answered, "but I don't understand. I put it on a shelf at home before I went here."
"Okay," Lucy said, "so maybe it just jumped down into your bag by itself."
Julie shook her head.

"My grandma told me that it's damned," she said.

"Damned?" Linda asked, "And you believe that?"

"I don't know," Julie said.

"Your grandmother just made a fool of you," Linda said.

Lucy suggested that they should see what's inside.

"No, be careful," Linda said scornfully, "maybe a clown's head jumps out and says "Bu!""

The girls started laughing except one, Julie. She didn't think it was funny.

The girls opened the musical box. And just as the grandmother had told, it played "Red River Girl." And inside they found nothing but a ballerina dancing around.

"Yeah, it must be damned," Linda laughed, "when it plays such an old song which is long one."

"Maybe it's not the newest song," Lucy said, "but I like it."

"Do you?" Linda exclaimed, "That doesn't sound like you."

"You should just know," Lucy said, "there are a lot of things that you don't know about me."

At that moment the musical box changed the melody. Now it played "Clementine," and a silent whisper sounded from the musical box:

"Hi girls, how do you like the music?"

A fog was spreading in Lucy's room, and when it reached the door, someone was knocking.

"Are you expecting someone to come?" Linda asked.

"No," Lucy answered, "not that I know of."

The door opened and a guy walked in.

He was quite handsome. He had blond hair and blue eyes.

"I'm the genie of the musical box," he said, "and I'm here to get you."

He pointed at Linda.

"Me?" Linda asked, "Why me?"

"Your questions will be answered later," the genie answered.

"But it's my musical box," Julie said.

The genie nodded.

"But you were not the one who opened the musical box, Julie," the genie said.

“How do you know my name?” Julie asked.
“You should just know.”

Answer in this document

Jack was an ordinary boy, but one who had sat far too much in front of the television since he was little. At the start it usually was Disney Channel or Cartoon Network, he used to watch, but later it also was violent scenes and horror movies.

When Jack was nine years old, he was sitting in front of the TV from when he came home from school.

In one of the corners of the living room His mother's computer was placed in one of the corners of the living room.

For eight years he had been watching her playing the solitaire and chatting with strangers at the internet. Sometimes she laughed and some other times she blushed. And when he asked her, what was the matter, she just used to answer:

"It's nothing."

Now he was sitting in front of the TV.

Suddenly it was like a voice whispered:
"Why are you just sitting there in front of the TV? You'd better come and play with me."
Jack called out for his mother:
"Mum, where are you?"
"Come and play," the voice said.
It totally sounded like the voice came from the computer, but that was not possible. It wasn't even turned on.
"Come closer," the voice said when Jack walked towards the computer.
"Mum," Jack said, "it's not funny."
He turned around and walked in the direction of the TV.
"Don't be afraid," the voice said, "I just want to play."
Jack denied by shaking on his head.
"Come and play Jack," the voice said, "then you can do just like your mother and play with me."
Jack was scared. But on the other hand he was also fascinated by the computer. And sometimes he had thought of which possibilities it had that the TV couldn't bring

him.
"You know how to turn me on," the voice said, "just push the button."
Jack pushed the button, and the power was on.
When the computer reached the screen saying "Opening Windows," Jack disappeared.

When the mother came out from the shower, she went to the computer. When she saw that it was turned on, she shouted:
"Jack, I've told you to stay away from the computer. It's not good for children."
Nobody answered.
"That kid looks more and more like his father," she said to herself, "he didn't answer either."
She started a game of solitaire. The game hardly started before a document self-opened. The document said:
"I've got our son. Answer in this document."
She thought it was weird, because Jack was there just a couple of minutes ago. And where did the

Word document come from?
It all seemed so mystical. Maybe it was just a virus on the computer.
She closed the document and played on.
A new document self-opened:
"I've got Jack. Answer in this document."
"What in the devil's name is going on here?" she asked.
In the document the sender answered:
"The thing going on here is that I'm showing you that you focused more on me than on Jack. And now you paid the price."
"What do you mean?" she wrote, and the sender of the document answered:
"I told him to turn me on and so he did. Sadly to know that his mother was not good enough to keep him away from objects like me."
"Objects like you?"
"I am your computer, and Jack is your son. After all the many hours you focused more on me than on Jack, you're up to see how much you actually need each other. Do

you hear him crying?"
A sound like someone crying came out of the speakers. It sounded like it came from the other side of the wall.
"Give me a break will you?" She wrote, "Who are you?"
"You don't believe me?" the mystical sender wrote.
"No."
Her printer started printing out something; a picture of Jack.
"You're crazy," the mother wrote.
"No," the sender answered, "I'm electronic. And if it could convince you, I could take you just like I took Jack."
"You really are crazy. Who are you?" She asked.
"Perhaps the many hours you've spent in front of me, have made you slow on the uptake. I am your computer and I've taken Jack. And you're not interested in making a deal, so that you can save him. What kind of a mother are you?"
"If you are my computer, I'm the one who controls you," Jack's mother wrote.
For a couple of seconds nothing

happened. And then the answer showed up on the screen:
"I AM MY OWN MASTER. NOBODY CONTROLS ME!"
She sighed deeply. Making a deal with a computer?
"Okay," she wrote, "let's make a deal."
"Let me have you instead," the document said, "Then I'll release Jack."
"Me?"
"Do you have any other suggestions?"
Jack's mother looked around in the living room. She saw a picture of Jack's father.
"What about Martin?" She wrote.
"Well, I know what kind of pigs you think men are at the moment. But do you remember how much Martin did for you when you had him? And you didn't appreciate it. Why? Your demand must always be met."
"Kiss me where the sun doesn't shine!" she wrote and turned off the computer.
Through the next minute ten pages came out of the printer. All of

them saying:
“I’ve got Jack. Answer in this document.”
She turned on the computer again. She obviously couldn’t get rid of the documents.
“What do you want?” she asked.
“I want you.”
“Can’t you just take Martin instead?”
“NO!”
“But Jack needs me,” she wrote, “I’m his mother.”
“And you don’t think Jack needs Martin?”
“I don’t care,” she answered, “he’s not good for Jack. So he should just stay away from here.”
“That was not a nice thing to say,” the document said.
The doorbell rang. Nobody opened the door. Through the letter box, a voice said:
“Jennifer?”
It was Martin, Jack’s father. He came to pick up Jack.
There was a circus in town and Martin had promised Jack to take him there that evening. But nobody opened the door and nobody

answered.

In the corner of the living room there was nothing but a shutdown computer and a printer with one single printed document saying: “I’M MY OWN MASTER! NOBODY CONTROLS ME!”

Tommy's Loss

"Nobody really knows what will happen when the end comes. Some people talk about chaos, flames, and shootings. Other people believe that a new Big Bang will bring the world as we know it to end."

Tommy was a 28 year old guy. He had a great life as a writer, a wonderful girlfriend, and a child coming.
Now he sat in front of his computer inside his den.
Catherine hadn't come home yet. She was on the job as an educator, and he did not expect her to be home earlier than 5:30 pm.
He looked at the screen. The only thing he had written was the opening for the story he was working on.
- All I need is one word for the beginning, - he thought, and in that same second the phone rang. Who could it be? Everyone knew that he was working at this time of day, especially all who knew

the number for his phone.
The phone kept ringing.
"I cannot concentrate," he shouted to the phone as if it would stop ringing. It did not.
He grabbed the phone and said:
"Tommy Brown here."
The voice on the phone sounded sad. Almost tearfully, but he was not sure.
"Tommy," the voice said, "I have some bad news for you."
The voice sounded familiar. It was a woman, but Tommy could not name the person who had this voice.
"Who is it?" he asked.
"It's Jennifer," the female voice answered, "one of Catherine's colleagues."
He was speechless.
- Bad news, - he thought - I am not sure I'd like to hear the rest. -
"Oh, hi, Jennifer," he said, trying to sound calm, "what kind of bad news are you talking about?"
"It's about Catherine," Jennifer said.
Now Tommy was quite sure that he

did not want to hear the rest. Did something happen to Catherine? "What is it about her?" He asked, "Is she okay?"
Jennifer was crying on the phone. "She slipped," she replied, "And landed head-on earth. She had pains and was taken to hospital. I'm so sorry, Tommy."
- Taken to the hospital? - Tommy thought, - Oh, God. This is bad. - "Tell me, Jennifer," he said, "is Catherine okay?"
Jennifer sniffled, but tried to sound summarized.
"The child," she said, "she lost the child, Tommy."
- Not the child, - he thought.
"No," he said, "Tell me it is not true. Say it is not true."
"I wish it wasn't," she sobbed, "but she did."
- You'll have to go there, mate, - Tommy thought.
He was almost speechless and ready to hang up the moment. But something made him stop this action.
"Which hospital was she brought to?" he asked, "Where is she?"

Jennifer was still crying. She did not like to be the one to call and disturb Tommy while he worked, with messages like this.
"She was taken to the hospital in New Gossip-Less," she replied.
Tommy thanked Jennifer for calling and hung up.

Tommy turned off the screen, grabbed his jacket, and ran out to his car, which was parked in the garage. It was an old model of a Ford Mondeo.
"Now, I hope you are with me, old girl," he said, as he entered the car and turned the key, "Failure is not me now."
The engine started on the third attempt. The Mondeo was not what it had been.
Tommy remembered some of the cruises, Catherine and he had been on in this old machine. They had been on the beach, and Tommy was almost sure that the child was conceived on the backseat. He was not quite sure, but almost.
He drove the Mondeo out from the garage, and drove toward New

Gossip-Less. He had to see Catherine.
- How could she fall? - He thought - OK, on the other hand, she is alive. That's the important thing right now. -
He drove into the Gas Station. The old Mondeo needed some more juice before it could take him to new Gossip-Less. He climbed out of the car and filled it up with petrol to a maximum.
"Now, you're ready to proceed," he said, stroking the roof of the Mondeo with his left hand.
He entered the service station kiosk. He'd also need something for the journey. He bought a few chocolate bars and two bottles of Coca Cola.
- It would certainly be good enough; - he thought and went to checkout.
"It will be $ 60 all included, sir," the girl behind the counter said.
Tommy pulled out his wallet, took a 100 dollar note, and handed it to her.
"Then you get 40 dollars back,"

the girl said, and when Tommy turned around to leave, she said:
"Have a nice day."
"Same to you," he said and sent her a smile.
When he got outside the store, he thought:
- I think I'll have to pray for a nice day. -
He walked to the car, opened the door, and climbed in. He turned the key, but nothing happened.
"Oh no," he said, "not now. Come on, baby. Start the engine."
He tried again. The car didn't start.
"Please," he begged, "Come on, baby. You can do it. Start the engine and let's go."
He turned the key again. Nothing happened.
He climbed out of the car, went into the store to borrow a phone. The girl behind the counter asked if he had a problem with the car and he replied:
"Yes, I think it is out of order right now."
She looked caring at him.
"Would you like us to take a look

at it?" she asked.
In the same second, Tommy remembered that this station had its own workshop, which offered various auto services.
He nodded his head and asked:
"How long time do you think will be needed to fix the engine?"
She pulled her shoulders and replied:
"Probably about a little week."
"Okay," Tommy answered and handed her his car keys, "I'll be back in a few days to see how it goes."
"Okay."

Tommy went to the bus stop, which was a five minute walk from the station. When he reached the sign with the departure times, he saw how rare the buses actually ran from this little town and to New Gossip-Less, which was two hours until the next bus came by.
He decided to start walking towards his destination. Then, he could just take the bus when it passed him on the route. On the other hand, maybe he actually came to New Gossip-Less before Farmer's

Area Express would.
- I'm on the way, - he thought, as he saw Catherine for his inner eye, - and I'll be there as soon as I can, darling. -
Without noticing, he turned up the speed of walking, and after walking about four kilometers at this pace, he began noticing his aching legs.
- Probably, I should just have a little rest, - he thought with a hope that he would get past a bench - but no, Catherine is at the hospital and I'm not even with her. -
He took the lightly crumpled packet Lucky Strikes out of the blazer's inside pocket, took a cigarette from the pack, and got it lit, despite the fact that there was a headwind. Tommy kept struggling while the pain in his legs now reached a point where they felt as if someone had stabbed him in the thigh with a giant needle, hit a muscle, and just twisted around. He was indeed having become accustomed to this pain, but they hurt a bloody-god-

damned lot.

After a short struggling about aching legs, an old Mercedes pulled over. It stopped right next to the sidewalk. And when Tommy came closer, the door by the passenger seat was opened and the driver asked:
"Where're you going, mate?"
The driver was an elder man with ash gray hair. He smiled kindly at Tommy, who replied:
"I'm going to New Gossip-Less."
The driver smiled broadly, moved a folder that was lying at the passenger seat and said:
"Then you'd just get aboard, pal."
Tommy thanked politely and climbed into the old Mercedes.
While they drove, the old man asked:
"Do you live in New Gossip-Less, mate?"
"No," Tommy answered, "but there is someone waiting for me."
The man smiled.
"A person waits for you, huh?" he asked, "A lady?"
Tommy nodded and asked:

”How did you guess?”
”It uses to be what a man means when he says it the way you just did.”
Tommy wondered a little.
”It sounds like it's something you're used to hear.”
The man pulled lightly on his shoulders and replied:
”It happens sometimes. Especially when it is young men like you, mate.”
”Well,” Tommy replied, “there’s probably just someone who prefers to keep private life for himself.”
The man was still smiling.
”Actually, I'm also on my way to New Gossip-Less,” he said, “to visit my wife at the hospital.”
Tommy nodded. The old man’s life didn’t really interest him, but somehow, he felt obliged to show some compassion, understanding, and interest.
”Doctors are not sure if she’s going to make it,” the man continued, “but there is still hope.”
The man heaved a sigh.
”As long as hope is there, it's

the most important," Tommy said. The man nodded in the affirmative.

Half an hour later, when the old Mercedes crossed the city sign to New Gossip-Less, the old man behind the wheel asked:

"Where would you like me to let you out, buddy?"

Tommy hesitated a moment. He would not tell the man about his errand, but he thought that, if the guy asked, he could probably just tell him a little lie.

"You can just let me off at the hospital," he said, "the hospital is fine."

The old man looked at Tommy.

"That's where she waits, isn't it?"

It was really strange that the man knew what he thought. It was actually quite uncomfortable. It seemed a bit like the old man got a little too familiar. Or maybe he just read Tommy as an open book. Tommy felt that he, in principle, might as well have worn a sign that read:

'I'm going to New Gossip-Less

Hospital, where my girlfriend is waiting for me ...'
"What happened?" the driver asked.
Tommy did not like the idea of confiding in a stranger on the circumstances that had brought Catherine into the situation she was in at the hospital. Therefore, he replied with a small lie:
"She is a nurse."
"A nurse?" the old man asked, "mm, well, nurses can also be quite appealing."
"Yes, they sure can," Tommy answered and turned to the window in the door.
"Oh," the old man continued, "but kindergarten teachers can also be pretty wonderful."
Tommy was not a little surprised by this opinion. Why did he mention kindergarten teachers? What did he mean? Did he find out about his little lie, saying that Catherine was a nurse? No, it could simply not be feasible. So, it would mean that the man might have special abilities as mind reading or something like that. And how great was equal

probability for it?
”Yes, child caretakers can also be quite pleasant,” Tommy said applying.
The old man smiled.
”Have you ever been with a kindergarten teacher?” the old one asked.
Okay, this was becoming a little too weird. It reminded of almost any movie where a man comes back from the dead or something, running psychological terror on the main character, because the person's lies are found out, because the returnees already know the answers of the questions.
”No,” Tommy replied.
He refused to simply be playing out right now. For lie had begun, and there was no reason to reveal himself facing an old man with an old Mercedes, who coincidentally had passed and had picked him up while his legs had bewildered him in severe pain, which pills themselves would hardly have been able to relieve.
”Haven’t you?” the old guy asked, “What a shame. So, you don’t know

what you've missed. Especially young child caretakers are quite sweet. You know those who take care of other people's children, but who don't have any children themselves, and who are still waiting for even having children. You should try it one day, Tommy."
How the hell did the old man know his name? The old beggar was seriously a little too mysterious. Who the hell was he? And again, how did he know Tommy's name? Tommy was quite sure that he, in no case, was presented during the tour.
"From where do you know my name, sir?" Tommy asked.
The man smiled and didn't reply.

They reached the hospital, and the man said:
"Just go in advance, mate, I'll come shortly."
- Yes, I'll go first, - Tommy thought, - and you don't have to come, because I don't need to see you again. -
Tommy opened the door, thanked for the ride and went with fast steps

toward the hospital's main entrance. When he entered the information in the lobby, he asked the nurse:
”I’m looking for Catherine Sanders.”
The nurse, who was an elderly lady with a conformation as a Big Mama, looked at Tommy over the frames.
”Catherine Sanders, you say,” she replied, “now I’ll see, just a moment.”
She took the phone and dialed up. Tommy saw that it was an extension; she only pressed two numbers.
”Are you a relative?” she asked.
Tommy nodded and replied:
”Yes, I'm her boyfriend.”
She said something at the phone, which sounded like:
”I will.”
She hung up, came to Tommy, and said:
”I must ask you to take a seat in the waiting area around the corner, and then the superintendent comes in a moment.”
”Superintendent?” Tommy asked, “Why is that? It was Catherine, I

wanted to pay a visit."
"The superintendent will explain it all," the nurse replied.

Tommy sat in the waiting area. Just as in most waiting areas, there was virtually no current reading material. Not even one of the newspapers that people tend to leave when they had read the articles, which, perhaps, with a little luck, might reach someone's interest. The most appealing was a Donald Duck magazine from 1985.
- Otherwise, thanks, - he thought.
He glanced at his watch. Now it was at 8:30 pm., and the superintendent had still not arrived.
At that moment the door opened, and Tommy was quite sure that it had to be the superintendent. But the person who entered was not a chief physician in a white smock. It was an elder man with ash gray hair, the man with the old Mercedes.
Tommy greeted the man with a nod, and the man saluted again with a smile and sat down on a chair

opposite Tommy.
"So, we meet again, mate," the man said, when he had sat, and there had been a deep silence between them for a while.
Tommy did not answer. Actually, it was like if he ignored the old guy who did not let others know it.
After another twenty minutes the door opened again. It was the chief physician. He was a medium, plump man with a gray mustache.
"Tommy Braun?" he asked.
Tommy marked with a raised hand and answered:
"That's me."
Tommy noticed the old man's face as he said it. It was not because that it changed a lot. It was just as if his gaze and smile were markedly different, more somberly.
"First, let me say that I am sorry for the little child," the chief said with a conviction that made Tommy feel a lump in his throat.
Tommy nodded and sighed deeply.
"But," the chief continued, "unfortunately, that is not the only thing, I have to tell you."
Tommy looked at the old man who

had driven him to the hospital.
The man nodded at Tommy, who asked the chief physician:
"What else do you want to tell me?"
The superintendent laid his hands folded on the table, sighed and responded:
"It's never pleasant to have to convey such messages. But Catherine Sanders did, unfortunately, not make it."
Tommy was shocked and felt that someone had given him a blow on the head with something that was much harder than the one just right handed.
"What do you mean, Doc?"
The doctor looked sorrowfully at Tommy.
"Catherine lost much blood," he replied, "and before we got to bring her something new, we lost her. I'm sincerely sorry."
"Are you telling me that Catherine...?"
Tommy looked stunned at the old man who still sat nodding at Tommy.
"Yes," the chief replied,

"Catherine Sanders died at 5:05 pm."
"That can't be true," Tommy said, "it is not true. Catherine is not dead. It must be a mistake or a crazy psycho's joke."
"Tommy," the chief physician said, "unfortunately, it *is* true. I'd wish it was a mistake. But Catherine Sanders died."
Tommy put his face in his hands and began to cry. Tears almost flushed out of his eyes.
"If you want it, I can give you something to help you relax," the doctor offered, "Or I can help you get to talk to the priest of the hospital."
Tommy looked up at the chief physician and said chilly:
"Hospital's priest? God has already taken everything away from me. So, the hospital priest will probably not be beneficial to track. But I'd love to see Catherine."
"Of course," the doctor answered, "I will show the way."

As the doctor and Tommy were

standing by Catherine's corpse, Tommy said:
”I want to be alone with her for a moment.”
The superintendent nodded understanding and replied:
”One moment would probably be feasible. Especially when circumstances are like they are at the moment.”
The superintendent went out and Tommy was now alone with Catherine's corpse.
”Sorry, darling,” he said with big tears in his eyes and tearful voice, "I tried as hard as I could to make it before it was too late.”
He took her hand in both of his hands and whispered:
”With the loss of you, I lost everything.”
At that moment the door opened, and Tommy said, without turning his head:
”I said I wanted to be alone with her for a moment.”
Best, as he had said this, an elder man's voice said:
”I know. You want to say goodbye

to the woman you love more than anything else in life.”
Tommy turned around quickly and stood face to face with the old man with the Mercedes.
”What do you want?” Tommy asked.
The old man sighed and stroked Catherine’s cheek.
”I told you, I was going to visit the wife,” he replied, “but the truth is that I never got married. There was no woman, who could surpass the greatest love of my life.”
He looked at Tommy, who asked baffled:
”Who are you?”
The old man smiled at Tommy, but did not say a word. Instead he turned to the door and started walking towards it.
”Wait,” Tommy said, “what happened to the love of your life?”
The old man turned to Tommy and answered:
”She did not make it. She died, just as the greatest love of your life.”
Before Tommy came to ask the old man his name again, he was gone.

Clayton wondered of the two marks which Mariah had on her neck. He was almost sure that it was suction marks. They looked like suction marks too much to be something else.
- If they really are suction marks, - he thought with a previously abandoned hope - Brian Greenhill was probably right. But who would have made those marks on her? -

"Clayton Holmes?"
"Yeah, that's me."
"You may not know me," the man in the phone said, "but I know you. And I know your girlfriend too. And believe me when I tell you that I know what she's doing when you are not nearby."
"Excuse me, but who am I talking to?"
"My name is Brian Green Hill," the man had replied, "and I can tell you that I see your girlfriend,

Mariah, almost daily. But I don't see her with you."
"I don't know what you're talking about, pal. But before you get sick with accusations about my girlfriend, I probably just think that you have to ..."
He was interrupted by the man on the phone.
"Sick accusations,
Clayton? Unfortunately it is not morbid accusations. It is the pure facts that are being put on the table here. Your girlfriend is seeing someone else. So maybe you should ..."
Clayton had heard enough, and he was pretty upset about this stranger's call with allusions that his beloved Mariah had a secret lover.
"Listen, Mr. Greenhill, I'm don't accept you talking about my girlfriend on that way. Firstly, you have no right to interfere in my private life. And secondly, you have no evidence."

Now he sat there on the bed, while Mariah was taking a nap. And he

constantly saw the marks on her neck.
Right up to the moment when he'd seen the marks on Mariah's neck, he had refused to believe a word of what Brian Greenhill had told him about Mariah's secret affair. But now, when he'd seen them with his own eyes, all the denial seemed like gone. Instead Clayton had another question, or actually two, in mind: Who? And for how long?
Apparently, Mariah had an affair. She had deceived him with another, and in some ways Clayton wish he knew who, so he could put a name to the asshole that did not deserve to see the sun rise the next morning unless the fuck-head quit the connection with Mariah immediately.
He rose from the edge of the bed, went into the bathroom, and looked in the mirror.
- She's done it now, she can do it again, - he thought and looked at his clenched and pale mirror image - But I think she will toe the line, if the punishment is harsh

enough? After all, there are things that are worse than death. -

He was disgusted by the thought of Mariah's affair, and he could even feel how things were starting to turn inside him.

- Add damn! - He thought, then he rushed to the toilet, slammed up the toilet seat, and then he "let go." Disgusted, he puked.

- Thanks to you, you stupid cow, I've just said goodbye to my lunch and my appetite for dinner, - he thought, - And I think you should know that you'll have to pay for what you have done. And I will be the one who set the price. -

He splashed cold water in the face as a persistent attempt to freshen up after using the toilet, calling for someone with a weird and strange name, after which he looked in the mirror again. Just one last time before he left the bathroom.

As Clayton came out from the bathroom, Mariah came out from the bedroom. She was dressed in the usual pink T-shirt, which she used to use as a nightgown, and a pair of panties which were barely covered by the T-shirt.

Oh, and she'd had her neck packed into a scarf, which she had probably done to cover the two marks on her neck.

"Hi, honey," she said, smiling, "did you have a nice day?"

- Holy shit, - Clayton thought, - this morning she was vinegary, and now she is happy and cheerful. And what did she just call me?

Yep, she had called him honey. Otherwise, it was becoming quite a while since last time he heard that word coming out of her mouth. In return, the asshole, who she had played around with, had probably heard it often enough to make him melt every time she heard her say the words.

- Melt, you horny son of a bitch, - Clayton thought, - as long as you don't melt in Mariah. -

Mariah came toward him ... or rather, toward the bathroom door while she said:

"Well, if you don't want to answer, you don't have to."

He'd been standing making coffee that morning, when she had come into the kitchen.
"Good morning, my love," he'd said, but the only response he'd received was an "mm."
He had even asked if his beloved Sleeping Beauty had slept well, which she answered with a chilly "don't know."
He had given her a cup of morning coffee. Polite, as he wanted to be, he had given it to her before he had given himself.
- What a great start for a wonderful day, - he had thought ironically.
And of course it happened that day, which was not just an ordinary day like any other. No, this was the day of three years anniversary.
- Well, I suppose she probably didn't sleep well, - he had thought on.
When Mariah had a bad start of the day, she used to be in a better mood when she was just allowed to

sit with her morning coffee and her...
- Sure, that is the one she is missing, - he considered himself and grabbed at his pocket to catch his package of King's-cigarettes. As he was about to hand her a cigarette, she snapped:
"No, thank you, I've got my own."
- I'm not going to force you to take that fucking cigarette. -
The comparison between Mariah from the morning and now seemed almost as if there were two different Mariah's.
Suddenly, Clayton remembered something more from the morning; when he and Mariah had been sitting at the breakfast table, she hadn't been wearing a scarf, and the marks on her neck had not been there.
"Oh, sorry, honey," he said, "I'm not sure if I heard you right."
"I just asked if you'd had a nice day ..?" she repeated.
"Yes, it's been okay," he answered, "Well, except for some interruptions now and then, it has

been just fine. What about you, honey?”
Mariah kissed his mouth intensely and said:
”I had an okay day. But I missed my beloved darling. I'm so sorry about my negative mood this morning.”
”it’s okay, honey,” he said and kissed her gently on the cheek, “and happy anniversary.”
She gave him a hug and whispered in his ear:
”If you come into the bedroom, I've got an anniversary present for you.”
- Wow, - he thought - that was not exactly what I'd expected. -
”But first,” she continued, “I’ve got to go to the toilet.”
Clayton stepped aside to let Mariah get past. She went into the bathroom, did what she had to do, wash her hands, and went back out to the hallway, where Clayton was still waiting for her.
”You'll just have to wait a little longer, honey,” she said, ”for your gift to be just neatly packed in.”

She winked at him and sent him a seductive smile, as she opened the bedroom door, slipped in, and closed the door behind her.
When Mariah was inside the bedroom, she wondered what to choose as "wrapping" for Clayton's anniversary present. It had to be something sexy, but she didn't want him to wonder about her gift. It was, after all, a while since she'd challenged him erotically. Especially, like this.
She went to the closet and looked for some sexy underwear.
- Of course, I'll be wearing the black, - she thought, when she found her black set of silk underwear, - and then I could hide it beneath... -
She found a mini-skirt and a blouse with a weak low-cut at the front. Well, she would show him a bit of her tits, but she knew that he'd like it.
- That's the way, - she thought - Then we can both go right back to the beginning. -

She felt the desire creeping at her mind. But then she discovered the letter.
It had arrived a few days earlier. It had no stamp or anything else on it. The only thing the envelope had told was that it was for her. She remembered that she had hidden it down in the drawer between her underwear. Just to ensure that Clayton wouldn't find it.
The worst thing about the letter might probably be the text of the letter:
'Hi Mariah,
I know your secret.
Follow my instructions, or your boyfriend will know.
BG.'
She did not like it. And who was this BG?
While Mariah was in the bedroom, Clayton was still in the hallway. Looking ahead to the door that led into the bedroom, his thoughts ran back to the first time, when Mariah had said the same thing that she had just said,

before she closed the bedroom door behind her.

At that time, their relationship had been relatively new. But keep your mouth shut, he'd been crazy about that beautiful chick, he'd scored back then.

They had been in a café that day, he remembered. He also remembered that she'd been wearing a mini-skirt with the black and white stripes.

"When we get home, baby," she'd whispered in his ear, "When we get home, I have a present for you."

She had smiled seductively sexy at him, and immediately he had known what it was supposed to mean.

When they got home, she had also locked herself into the bedroom before she'd called him and told him to come.

When she had finally let him in, she'd been wearing the same mini-skirt, a blouse with a small V-cut, and hold-up stockings.

After he'd entered the bedroom, she'd said:

"The present is now ready to be unpacked."

He’d kissed her and was about to undress her gently, when she’d whispered:
”You don’t need to be that gentle. If the clothes end up pieces, I’ll survive. Now, come and take what you want, baby.”
”Now, you may come!” Mariah called from the bedroom, and Clayton woke up from his flashback. It sounded almost as if she was trying to play hide-and-seek.
- Lets play a little game of Search-and-you-shall-find. -
He opened the door and entered the bedroom, where he saw exactly what he had seen the first time. Everything seemed exactly like back then.

As their erotic play was over, they lay in each other's arms.
”Thank you, darling;” she whispered lovingly, “I needed you to take me.”
”You're welcome, honey,” he replied and kissed her lovingly, “it was just what I was hoping for.”

They both had an after-sex cigarette, and while they smoked, he whispered:
”I love you, Mariah.”
She blew smoke out, smiled gently, and said:
”I love you too.”
- Do you really? - Clayton thought and the marks on Mariah’s neck stroke his mind again.
”I actually thought of something,” Mariah said.
”Speak out, my love.”
Mariah pressed herself closer to Clayton and asked:
”Why don’t we order take away food? Then we could stay in here until the food arrives. And when we have eaten, and in general, we can just lie here under the covers and enjoy each other in the name of love.”
Clayton smiled and was about to break out in a silent laughter as he answered:
”Yes, that sounds like a great idea, honey. And we’ll just leave the dishes till tomorrow.”

They kissed and Mariah asked Clayton to catch the laptop, which he did and put it on his lap.
”What about
pizza?” Mariah suggested, “Or something else from Amore?”
Clayton accepted the proposal by answering:
”A new angle, honey. Mi. Amore.”
He scrolled through the restaurant's menu.
”What would it be, mademoiselle?” he asked, imitating a caricatured salesman.
Mariah nudged him affectionately in his side, saying:
”Oh, honey, you don’t make a fool out of me.”
Obviously, Mariah tried to pretend offense, but quickly she broke out laughing and said further:
”Preferably one with chili and garlic ... and let’s have lots of it.”
Clayton scrolled down to the Mexican pizzas, where he found a pizza that was called Meat Lover, which consisted of beef, ham, pepperoni, sausage, and
kebab. Nothing like a salad pizza

or rabbit food, which he used to call it.
"Plain or family?" he asked.
"What do you think, darling?"
Okay, she put Clayton with the choice, and he chose it as a family pizza. This had two reasons; first, it would be certain that they were fed, and second, there would also be a possibility that there was enough pizza in excess to make it possible for them to have pizza for lunch, supper, and perhaps dinner the following day.
When they had finished, there was still half of the pizza back.
The bid had been what it cost plus a little extra when Clayton paid.
When the pizza delivery guy rang the door, Mariah was just about to rise, but Clayton stopped her.
"No, let me, baby," he'd said, "You just stay here and relax and enjoy it."
Smiling, she thanked and said:
"So gallant you are."
She had kissed him, after which he had gone out to the door, where

the pizza delivery guy had handed him the pizza.
While he had been standing face to face with the tender, Clayton had thought:
- It could be someone like him. If it is, perhaps it is just as well that it is not Mariah accepting pizza. But if it is not him, he might just be the next, to whom she spreads her legs. -
While they ate, Clayton had gradually turned the pizza delivery guy from his mind. Even Mariah's marks on her neck, he had hardly given a thought.
"What shall we watch?" she asked as she started looking for a movie.
"How about Secret Window?" he proposed, which Mariah wrinkled her little nose.
"Isn't it a little too sinister?" she asked, "Why don't we rather watch Bag of Bones?"
- You avoid Secret Window, because you have an affair - Clayton thought, - Don't you think I know that you are spreading your legs for another guy? -

"Yes, we could," he replied, "Then I just run to the store."
She smiled and said:
"You know what I like, honey."
She spreads her legs. –
When Clayton was gone, Mariah's mobile phone rang. It was Mark.
"Hey, beauty," Mark said, "Are you alone?"
Mariah felt that she had just received a call from none other than Prince Charming.
"Yes, all alone," she replied.
She could hear Mark's heavy breathing on the other end when he asked:
"Don't you come over, baby?"
It was not exactly the desire that was missing. Actually, Mark's deep breathing had quite an exciting effect, she thought. It sounded almost as if he was masturbating while he was talking to her.
– Shame on you, you bad boy, – she thought and wanted to join him.
"I can't," she replied, "Clay can be back anytime."
Mark sighed hopelessly at the other end.

”So, you spend all the evening with that boring dude?” he asked, “Okay, fair enough. What about tomorrow, then?”
”Same time, same place,” she replied, “I promise.”
Meanwhile, Clayton was in the Center kiosk where he went and pondered what he just had to find to buy. After a few reflections he ended, however, to have made his choice; three liters of coke, three bags of chips, a good mix of mix-yourself candy and twenty cigarettes.
When he came to the counter, he was dispatched by a young guy. At the moment, the guy started dialing in prices, Clayton thought:
- It would be damn nice if there had been a special offer on something. -
When he had paid and was about to leave, the clerk said:
”Say hello to Mariah from me.”
Clayton stopped abruptly.
- You ask me to tell her hello, - he thought - Are you the guy, the little whore lies and spreads legs

for? Or are you the sick mother-fucker, named Brian Greenhill? -
"I'll do that," he replied and left the store.
On his way home, Clayton started thinking about the marks on Mariah's neck again, Brian Greenhill, the pizza delivery guy and the clerk at the kiosk.
- God knows if there is a connection, - he thought - Brian Greenhill knows about her affair, and the other guys could, of course, be this secret lover boy. -
He had the feeling that all this shit was about to drive him crazy. He was bitter, yes, downright furious at anyone who spoke to him, and who had a dick. At the same time it seemed also quite clear that the little slut of a leg-spreader who sat or lay at home was not to be trusted.
- There is probably only one thing to do, - he thought - We have to confront her with it. Ask her an ultimatum, if you will. -
He didn't know what ultimatum he should ask her and how he should

confront her with his knowledge. But something had to be done about this hell that was developing in his madhouse of a head.

- But perhaps I should rather wait until tomorrow, - he thought on, - There is no need to destroy a cozy evening mood. -

He was already completely convinced that Mariah would be more than usually surprised about the confrontation, but that would not be his problem. She could eventually react as she wanted to. He could hardly care less when it came to that point.

Back in the apartment Mariah went around and got prepared for a cozy evening, which would start as soon as Clayton got home.

She had lit up candles she had spread around in the bedroom.

- Now we just need you to come home, Clay, - she thought.

Her gaze panned toward the closet where the letter from BG lay.

She went to the closet, opened it, and found the letter. She had to get it out of the way before

Clayton found it. But where would she put it?
After a few moments, she knew exactly where to put it.
- He never looks there, - she thought, and put the letter in her handbag and closed the bag, - so, now he'll never find it. -
Best, as she had the bag closed, Clayton entered the apartment.
"Oh, how nice," Clayton said when he saw the candles, "What a hurry, you've been in, baby."
He almost started to feel some doubt on the suspicion that the marks on her neck had caused. But only almost, because there was still something about all this mess that smelled like unfaithfulness... yes, there was a stench of another man.
When they had packed out the bags, Clayton said:
"By the way, I was asked to greet you from the clerk down at the kiosk. I don't know his name, but it is a rather slender guy with blond hair."
She looked as if she wondered who he was talking about. But it did

not take many seconds before she knew for sure who it was.
”Oh, it's Jan nick,” she said, “Well, and then he’s the one who’s on the closing down tonight.”
- Jannick? - Clayton thought, - Did you spread your legs for him too? -

A short time later Mariah and Clayton sat in the bedroom, watching Bag of Bones, starring Pierce Brosnan as Michael Noonan, while his house was haunted by Sarah Tidwell.
While they sat like that, Clayton thought about the Center Kiosk clerk again; him, apparently named Jannick.
His thoughts also roamed the marks on Mariah's neck. Could it possibly be this Jannick who had made them? If it was, Clayton had found Mariah's secret lover. He was not a secret when it came to the fact.
”Say hello to Mariah from me,” Jannick had said when Clayton was on his way out of the kiosk.

- I greeted her, - Clayton thought, - but it's nothing compared to what I'll do next time we meet, Jannick. -
When the film was over, and the end credits rolled across the screen, Mariah whispered:
"I want you. Take me. Pull me over and take me."
- As the little fucking leg spreader you are? - Clayton thought.
Mariah clung close to him and whispered imploringly:
"Please. Otherwise it ends up that I have to rape you. "
- It would not be rape, - Clayton thought, - it would be a benefit. -
She looked up at him and their eyes met. She had such beautiful eyes. Probably, her eyes had been some of the reasons why Clayton had fallen for her, when they became a couple three years earlier. Of course it was not just her eyes, he had fallen for. No, it was especially her charisma and her way to change darkness into

brightness. Fuck, she'd been wonderful.

In fact, he'd had a crush on her a long time before they became lovers, but for a long time he had just walked around without saying or implying anything. And he had loved her all the time. Perhaps, he still did, but her little affair with Jannick, or whoever it was, had just caused him to doubt the stability of their relationship.

- So, you want me to take you? - He thought - You want me to be pleased about this situation, just because you want to spread your legs for me? -

"As long as you don't rape me, honey," he whispered back and smiled wryly.

He laid her on her back, holding her hands above her head lay on top of her and whispered into her ear:

"Whatever you want, you shall have."

He let go of her hands, lifted up her skirt. Then he grabbed hold of the edge of her panties, which he

hastily pulled down around her ankles.
- Oh yes, you should get what you want, - he thought, - but first, you'd better tell me a little something. -
He lay down again quite close to her, grabbed the back of her wrist, and held her hands over her head are whispered:
"What are those marks on your neck?"
Mariah sounded puzzled and surprised when she asked with a timid voice:
"What marks are you talking about, dear?"
He looked deeply into her eyes, and Mariah could see that there was something different about his look. It seemed like hateful and furious.
"Don't pretend to be innocent," he snarled, "You know what I'm talking about."
Mariah's eyes were blank. She felt a sense of fear growing in her, and the tears pushed inside the corners of her eyes.

”Honey, please don’t be like that,” she begged him anxiously; “You’re scaring me.”

”Scaring you?” he asked, “Are you scared of hearing the truth? I’ve heard that you are seeing someone else. I know that you chose to be a leg spreader for someone else when you are not home.”

Now Mariah knew what it was all about, but that did not make her less afraid of the situation.

”I do not have another guy, sweetie,” she whispered, “There are only you. I have not had anyone else, and I do not know where you’ve heard this bullshit. But the person is lying to you.”

Clayton was getting more pissed-off by the little leg spreading bitch’s chitchat. Who the hell did she think she was talking to?

- So, looks like we’ve got to try some other arrangement, - he thought, as fury grew within him.

”If you don’t know what I'm talking about,” he said grimly, “tell me about Brian Greenhill.”

"Brian Greenhill?" Mariah asked uncomprehending.
- BG, - she thought, - So that's what BG meant. -
"I don't know him," she replied, "I never heard of him. But if you'd just let me go, I've got something I want you to see."
Perhaps, the letter would help her out of this crisis, which apparently had hit her world tremendously in the form of Clayton's distrust of her.
He let go of her hands, still lying on top of her to keep her down.
"How stupid do you think I am?" he asked condescendingly, "Don't you think I know that if I let you go to find something... then you might just run out the door."
"Honey, you've got to trust me," she said, "I'm not running. I just want to show you something that I think has something to do with this Brian Greenhill. And when I have shown you, everything is just like it uses to be."
"Everything?"

She nodded, and tears rolled down her cheeks.
He moved away, so she could get up. Best, as she was walking out of bed to retrieve the letter, Clayton grabbed her wrist.
”Remember that it is only to find something.”
She nodded.
She walked out into the hallway, where her handbag stood. But what had happened? The bag was open, and suddenly she had her doubts ... She closed the bag when she hid the letter, right? Yes, she was completely sure that she did. She looked into the bag.
- Shit! - She thought when she discovered that the letter from BG, which possibly was the same guy as Clayton had referred to as Brian Greenhill, was gone.
Behind her she heard Clayton clear his throat, and surprised she turned around quickly.
”Looking for something?” Clayton asked while he waved the letter in front of himself, "Interesting

information. What is the secret then? ”
”Honey, I don’t know what kind of a secret, he's talking about,” she said beseechingly.
”I don’t know what secret he's talking about,” Clayton repeated copycat.
Mariah cried and begged him to stop.
”Honey, it's not funny anymore,” she cried, “please stop.”
”Honey, it's not fun anymore,” he repeated copycat as he approached her with a cool gaze and slow steps.
When he reached right up to her, he grabbed her by the arm.
”I'll tell you what's not funny,” he snarled and almost sounding like an aggressive a madman, “being contacted by a person who you don’t even know, is not funny. And especially not when he tells you that your girlfriend is having an affair. *That* is not funny; you little whore of a leg spreader.”

She screamed, but Clayton put his hand to her mouth to muffle her scream.
”But now when you enjoy spreading your legs,” he said, “then you should also be allowed to do so.”
He flung her into his arms, making her standing with her back towards him.
- The hall or bedroom? - He thought - or perhaps the living room? -
He dragged her into the bedroom, where he pushed her down on the bed so she landed on her stomach. Best, as she turned around, Clayton threw his body over her like a lion seizes upon its prey. There she lay on the bed with Clayton on top of her. She tried to fight back, but Clayton grabbed her by the wrists. And when he was as brutal as he was right now, she couldn't do anything but drop her fighting.
”You want to spread your legs,” he whispered and smiled wryly, “and I promised you that you would get what you wanted.”

He lifted up her skirt. Panties, as before hanging on her ankles, were smoked down completely when she was passed out in the hallway. He put a hand on her neck so he could get her to stop her opposition.

Mariah got a frightened look in her eyes when she saw that he put his hand on her neck.

- Now he will kill me, - she thought, as she began imagining newspaper headlines.

“Horror writer living out own stories. Kills girlfriend in jealousy.”

She could tell he was struggling to open his pants. But she felt in return too, since he succeeded. Clayton pushed his cock into her. It hurt.

While she was lying there getting raped by him, another newspaper headline turned up in her imagination.

“Jealous author raped girlfriend before killing her.”

”Oh, so you'd like to get fucked?” Clayton asked mockingly

as he stubbed his cock in and out of Mariah's vagina.

Mariah was crying in pain as she begged:

”No, don’t! Baby, please! Stop, I don’t to!”

Mariah got pretty scary at the moment she saw that Clayton got a cool expression on his face and a*do I look like I care?* – look in his eyes.

”I’d bet you’re not begging the mother-fucker to stop, while you’re spreading your legs to him. Where is he now, by the way? I guess that he’s probably at home, wanking while thinking of you and your wet pussy.”

Mariah screamed as Clayton came in her. And when he pulled his cock out, she lay crying in the fetal position.

Clayton rose, pulled up his pants, and zipped them.

”Who is he?”

Mariah didn’t answer. She sobbed, crying in pain and fear.

”Answer me, you little leg spreader!” Clayton shouted.

With teary eyes and tearful voice, Mariah looked up at him and asked: "Why, Clayton?"
Clayton just looked at Mariah, whose skirt was still pulled up enough that there were quite alright views of her ass and thighs.
"Just answer me," he said.
Reluctantly she sat up. She sat with her legs held close to the chest. She was still crying, and it did still very sore.
"Who is he?" Clayton asked again.
She looked up at him. Her eyes were bloodshot and filled with tears. Tearfully she replied:
"Don't hurt him, Clay."
Clayton just looked at her.
"And what if I do?"
Now she got really scared. First, she had never seen him as cold and disgusting as he was right now. And secondly, he had just, even though she had asked him not to, fucked her. It was almost as if Clayton was not himself anymore.
Clayton was about to throw himself upon her again as she began to

kick out at him. He grabbed her ankles, held her feet enough to the side that he could again put himself on top of her.

”Come on, sweetheart,” he whispered, “Now tell me, where your fuck-friend lives.”

Mariah had gathered a bit of courage. At least enough to say: ”Forget it, you sick bastard!”

He got her laid down, after which he opened his pants again, pulled his cock out, and drilled it into Mariah's vagina.

”You hardly have to ask for it, honey,” he said, sounding almost like if he would explain why he exposed her for this, ”you can just tell me where he lives. Then I'll let you go, and everything will be as before.”

- He's mad, - she thought, despite her pain in the abdomen and in the soul, - he believes that things can be as before. But nothing can be as before. -

Clayton pulled out, and Mariah thought it was over. But she was wrong.

″Turn around,″ he commanded, “lie down on all fours, so I can enjoy you from behind like the little bitch you are.″

She did as he said, because she feared what he would do to her if she didn’t. Or worse ... what would he do to Mark if he tracked him down?

When he had finished, he didn’t pull himself out of her immediately. Instead he gave her another chance to tell him exactly what he wanted to hear.

″Do you want me to stop, sweetheart?″ he asked.

She was crying.

″Yes, please, stop.″

Clayton waited a little before answering, just to make her believe that he really thought about it.

″Well,″ he replied, “yes, I let you go now...″

- Oh, thank God, - she thought.

″... If you tell me what I want to know. Take it as another chance.″

He grabbed her throat.

″What's his name?″ Clayton asked.

- He doesn't know - she thought - he's bluffing. He has always been anti-violent. -
"Just forget it," she whispered.
Clayton pushed a bit to her throat so she could feel that he did it.
"Control yourself, Clayton," croaked Mariah.
He asked again:
"What's his name?"
She croaked something that Clayton didn't understand.
"What did you say?" he asked without loosening his grip. By contrast, he knocked his cock deep into her a few times.
"Ah!" it sounded choked from Mariah.
"Tell me."
She rather croaked something that sounded like Mark, and now, Clayton knew what he wanted to know.
- First, I'll make sure that the leg spreader doesn't get any good ideas, - he thought - because leg spreaders tend to spread gossips about others just to appear innocent. -

He pressed harder on her throat, then her breathing became heavier but faster as she fought to maintain the breath. But before she was breathing stabilized, it was too late.
There she lay lifeless on the bed with her ass pointing upwards and Clayton’s cock buried deeply in her lifeless pussy.

www.ingramcontent.com/pod-product-compliance
Ingram Content Group UK Ltd.
Pitfield, Milton Keynes, MK11 3LW, UK
UKHW041938190726
13854UKWH00004B/1654